The Adventures of Bailey & Bernard

Bailey's Lost Ball

Written by Stacey A. Raymond
Pictures by Tanya Matiikiv

The Adventures of
Bailey & Bernard

Bailey's Lost Ball

Written by Stacey A.Raymond

Pictures by Tanya Matiikiv

This book is dedicated to my daughter,
Montana and all children who love books.

Archway Publishing books may be ordered through booksellers or by contacting:

Archway Publishing
1663 Liberty Drive
Bloomington, IN 47403
www.archwaypublishing.com
844-669-3957

ISBN: 978-1-6657-7231-0 (sc)
ISBN: 978-1-6657-7233-4 (hc)
ISBN: 978-1-6657-7232-7 (e)

Library of Congress Control Number: 2025901540

Print information available on the last page.

Archway Publishing rev. date: 2/21/2025

On a fine, sunny day, Bernard was enjoying
his routine flight.
Swooping through clouds, a white and gray figure
came into sight.

He spotted a familiar dog named Bailey.
She was running fast on the sand.
Bernard, continuing to follow, shouted,
"Hey there, you need a hand?"

As her paw prints were marking the beach, he was dodging clouds in the air.
Let it be known this sheepdog and seagull are a friendly little pair.

Halloween

Fishing Day!

Naps

Knowing his best friend so well, Bernard thought,
How can this be?
Bailey does not swim well, and now she is too close
to the sea!

Bernard was yelling, "Bailey! What are you doing so far from home?"

Bailey said, "I'm chasing my new red ball, but it is disappearing in the foam!"

From above, Bernard spied the ball bobbing up and down on a wave.
Bailey was thinking, Please be still, ball, then you'll be easier to save!

So close to the water,
Bailey was getting worried and very wet.
She was not too happy with this ball.
The ball she needed to get.

7

The flying sand and ocean spray began creating a problem for her hair.
All those shaggy clumps were making it hard to see.
It was quite unfair.

You see,
sheepdogs keep
their hair
long, protecting
their eyes from
the sun.

But sometimes,
when her hair
grows too long,
her mom ties it
up in a bun.

It was too late for hair tying, she was in another pickle. There was no time. No time to be fickle.

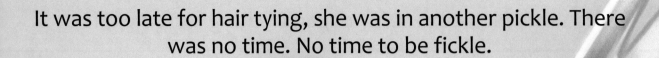

With the waves swishing and sloshing the ball was going too far.

Yelling from the sky, Bernard said, "I can get it with my guitar!"

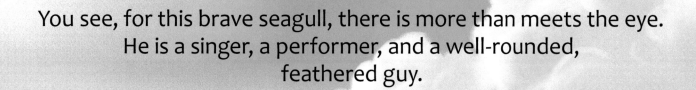

You see, for this brave seagull, there is more than meets the eye.
He is a singer, a performer, and a well-rounded,
feathered guy.

With his favorite guitar on his back, Bernard kept
eyeing the ball.
He was thinking, How should I get this? It's not going to be easy
at all!

This was not the first time he was helping his friend in a bind.
Since Bailey's so shaggy, for her, things were hard to find.

For example, this one time, after lounging on the beach.
Bernard spotted something stuck to her butt, just out of reach.

They laughed at the sight of it, and he quickly
began to assist.
He pulled the starfish from her butt and giggled.
He simply could not resist.

No matter the problem, he was always helping Bailey. He would be there for her whether it's monthly, weekly, or daily!

Now, he was getting close to the water, but the ocean was
swallowing her ball.
Bernard was struggling because the waves were
so very tall.

Helplessly waiting, Bailey could not see.
Where was Bernard? Her ball? She only saw the sea!

Finally, the waves began to calm, and Bernard was in sight!
She was so happy he was there. Wow, what a fright!

Like a golf pro, he was swinging his guitar,
while heading to shore.
He kept going and going until he could not go anymore.

Bernard, gasping for air, briefly sprawled on a wave to have a quick little float.

Before long, he was paddling so fast, like a small, feathered boat.

Crawling to the beach, Bernard tossed Bailey the ball.
Boy, was she happy to have it, but seeing her friend was the best
of all!

Bailey said, "Thank you so much, Bernard. I hope you are okay!"
He replied, "Why, of course, silly sheepdog,
it is just another day!"

Bernard feeling better, shook the water from each wing.
And then this talented little seagull, began
to spontaneously sing.

"My best friend is gray and white, just like me.
My best friend is a dog, and we both live by the sea.
Have you met my best friend? She is as shaggy as can be! Do you
know that my best friend has never had a flea!"

"Bailey is my best friend; she fills my heart with glee! Bailey is my best friend, so fluffy she can't see!
Bailey is my best friend, and she is a nut!
She's a fuzzy little duster and stuff sticks to her butt!"

Bailey was smiling and dancing, moving her shaggy feet to the beat.

The private little concert continued.
Bernard kept singing and playing guitar.

"My friend may be a dog, but she really is the best!
When she is in a pickle, I will be put to the test.
Silly, silly Bailey, I will ALWAYS help you out.
And I know you will need me again, without a single doubt!"

Bailey cheered
and smiled,
then gave her friend a
high five.
She was happy he was
a good swimmer
and made it out alive!

After the song,
Bernard flopped
on her back and
loudly sighed.
Bailey was about to do
his favorite thing,
taking him
for a sheepdog ride!

He sat on Bailey's back, holding her hair from her eyes.
He wanted her to see since he wasn't guiding from the skies.

The End.

About the Author

Stacey A. Raymond, originally from New York, is a writer and interior designer who resides by the beach in sunny Florida with her husband and
their Old English Sheepdog, Bailey.
Stacey is an avid reader, runner, and animal lover.
Her writings include a series of children's stories about a special friendship between a shaggy dog
and a singing seagull. On their adventures, the pair help each other, and seaside friends, in times of need.

Printed in the United States
by Baker & Taylor Publisher Services